For (begrudgingly) Maisie, Georgia, Felix,
Catherine, Casper, Alice, Kara, Jack, and Luke.
I did like being an only child but: the more, the merrier.
— L. S.

Rabbit! Rabbit! Rabbit!

LORNA SCOBIE

Henry Holt and Company
New York

I am the only child in my family,
and that is the way I like it.

The fox next door says she likes having rabbits around.

— The more, the merrier, she says.

But I can't see why.

I like having everything to myself.

My flower

My carrots

My
stretching
area

My bedroom

But my parents have some news.

Suddenly, I am no longer an only child.

Napping in my stretching area

In my bedroom!

I have to establish some rules.

This works well.

Until . . .

Something has to be DONE.

Then I remember the fox.

Would YOU look after these rabbits?

Gladly!

YESSSSSS!

It's just me!

Just . . . me?

I go next door.

Would you like
to come in, too?
The more,
the merrier.

Okay then, I guess.

And much to my surprise . . .

It is fantastic!

Henry Holt and Company, *Publishers since 1866*
Henry Holt® is a registered trademark of Macmillan Publishing Group, LLC
120 Broadway, New York, NY 10271
mackids.com

Library of Congress Cataloging-in-Publication Data is available
ISBN 978-1-250-76074-6

Our books may be purchased in bulk for promotional, educational, or business use. Please
contact your local bookseller or the Macmillan Corporate and Premium Sales Department
at (800) 221-7945 ext. 5442 or by email at MacmillanSpecialMarkets@macmillan.com.

Originally published in the United Kingdom in 2020 by Scholastic UK
First American Edition, 2021
Designed by Trisha Previte
Artist used ink pens, watercolor, and colored pencils.
Printed in China by RR Donnelley Asia Printing Soluations Ltd.,
Dongguan City, Guangdong Province

1 3 5 7 9 10 8 6 4 2